TO Baby Hudson ♡
∙∙∙∙∙∙∙∙∙∙∙∙∙∙∙∙∙∙∙∙∙∙∙∙∙∙∙∙∙∙

HAPPY
EASTER

Love Stacy, Jonny
Luke & Ava ♡
xoxo
∙∙∙∙∙∙∙∙∙∙∙∙∙∙∙∙∙∙∙∙∙∙∙∙∙∙∙∙∙∙

Can't wait to
meet you! You are
So loved already!
-xoxo-

D1569753

THE EASTER BUNNY
is coming to
PITTSBURGH

Written by Eric James   Illustrated by Mari Lobo

sourcebooks
wonderland

The sweet Easter Bunny
is skipping along,
heading through Pittsburgh
singing this song:

Cakes

ALLEGHENY
BOOKS

TINY THE
PITTSBURGH
EASTER BUNNY

The Littlest
Bunny in
Pittsburgh

"The eggs are delivered.
My Easter job's done.
And now it is time
that I joined in the fun!"

She jumps down a tunnel
that runs underground,
and pops up again
to look all around.

North Side, South Shore,
and Shadyside, too.
I bet there's a tunnel
that's very near you!

In Highland Park children have smiles on their faces, and eggs decorated like people and places!

RUFFED GROUSE PARK

But one little boy
drops the egg from his hands.
A loud **CRACKING** sound
can be heard as it lands.

"Oh dear!" says the bunny,
and dabs at a tear.
"You need cheering up
so thank goodness I'm here!"

She wiggles her ears,
she hops on the spot,
she waggles her tail,
and he giggles a lot!

In Squirrel Hill, there is
an Easter parade.
Most children are clapping
but one looks afraid.

That clapping is noisy.
These legs are so TALL!
It's crowded and loud,
and she's ever so small!

"Gee whiz, what a din!
I know just what to do.
Come here little one
and I'll hold hands with you!"

She wiggles her ears,
and spins her around.
The little girl laughs
as her feet leave the ground!

Down in Frick Park
while having a rest,
the bunny eats sweet Apple Pie.
(It's the best!)

Across in the park
there's an egg-rolling race.
A small boy falls down
and he's now lost his place!

The bunny trips up
as she's going to help.
She falls down the hill
with an **OUCH** and a **YELP!**

YELP!

OUCH!

She's just a big blur
as she tumbles on past.
The boy runs to help her.
He's going so FAST!

FINISH

She wiggles her ears,
he can't (but he tries!).
They hop up and down
for they've just won first prize!

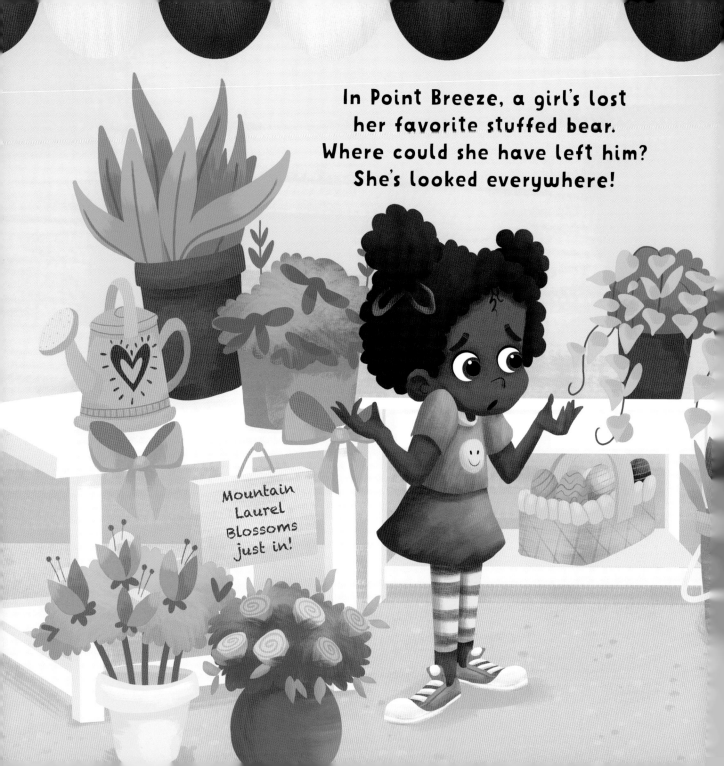

In Point Breeze, a girl's lost
her favorite stuffed bear.
Where could she have left him?
She's looked everywhere!

Mountain
Laurel
Blossoms
just in!

"When I'm feeling sad
do you know what I do?
I hop up and down!
Do you want to try too?"

She wiggles her ears, the girl thinks it's funny,
and laughs even more when she hops like a bunny!

They both jump around like they haven't a care.
And look what the chicks have just found, over there!

In Oakland, the bunny
helps children with SHARING.

In Greenfield, she helps a sweet child
to be DARING.

In Morningside she SINGS,
in Westwood she WIGGLES.

Wherever she goes
she brings LAUGHTER and GIGGLES!

This day's been so busy
but also such fun.
The bunny daydreams
in the warm setting sun.

The twilight is coming,
the three chicks are lazing,
and tweeting about
how this day's been #AMAZING!

More chocolate needs making!
New eggs will need wrapping!
It's all so exciting,
the three chicks start flapping!

"Pittsburgh is great and we love being here. We'll make lots more eggs and we'll be back next year!"

She wrinkles her nose,
she wiggles her ears,
she blows you a kiss,
and she just...disappears!

Written by Eric James
Illustrated by Mari Lobo
Additional artwork by Barbara Szepesi Szucs
Designed by Nicky Scott

Published by Sourcebooks Wonderland,
an imprint of Sourcebooks Kids
P.O. Box 4410, Naperville, Illinois 60567-4410
(630) 961-3900
sourcebookskids.com

Date of Production: August 2019
Run Number: 5015369
Printed and bound in China (1010)
10 9 8 7 6 5 4 3 2 1